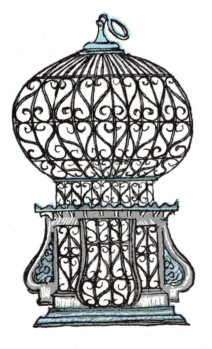

Why the Jackal Won't Speak to the Hedgehog

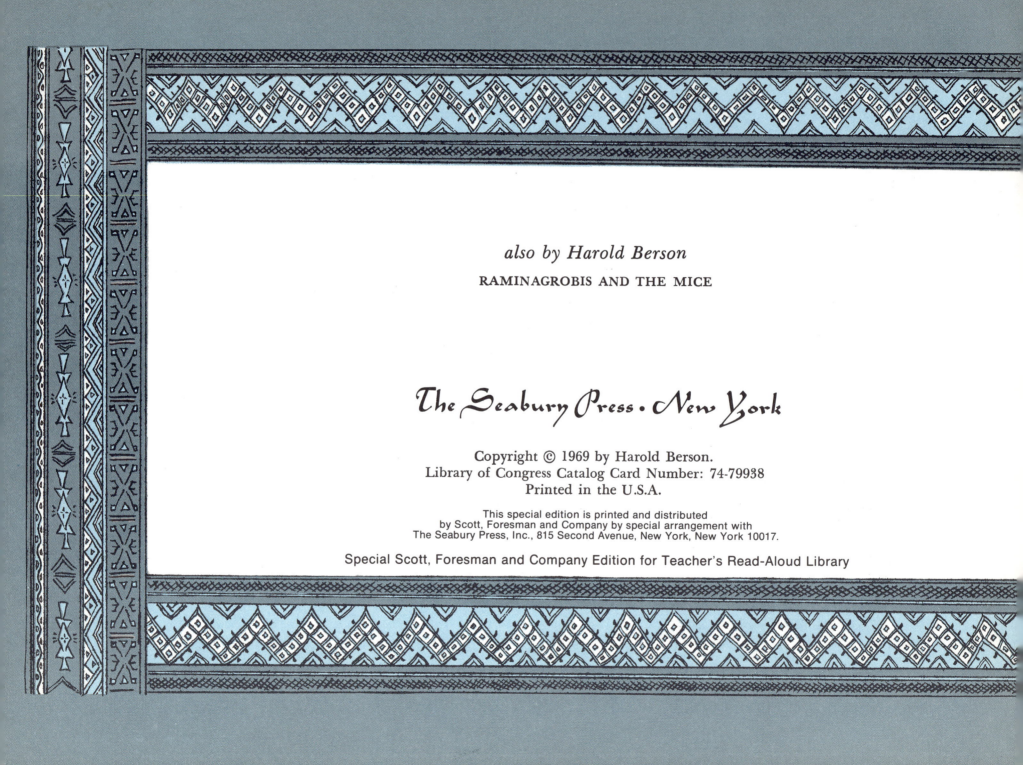

also by Harold Berson

RAMINAGROBIS AND THE MICE

The Seabury Press · New York

This special edition is printed and distributed
by Scott, Foresman and Company by special arrangement with
The Seabury Press, Inc., 815 Second Avenue, New York, New York 10017.

Special Scott, Foresman and Company Edition for Teacher's Read-Aloud Library

Why the Jackal Won't Speak to the Hedgehog

a Tunisian folk tale retold and illustrated by

Harold Berson

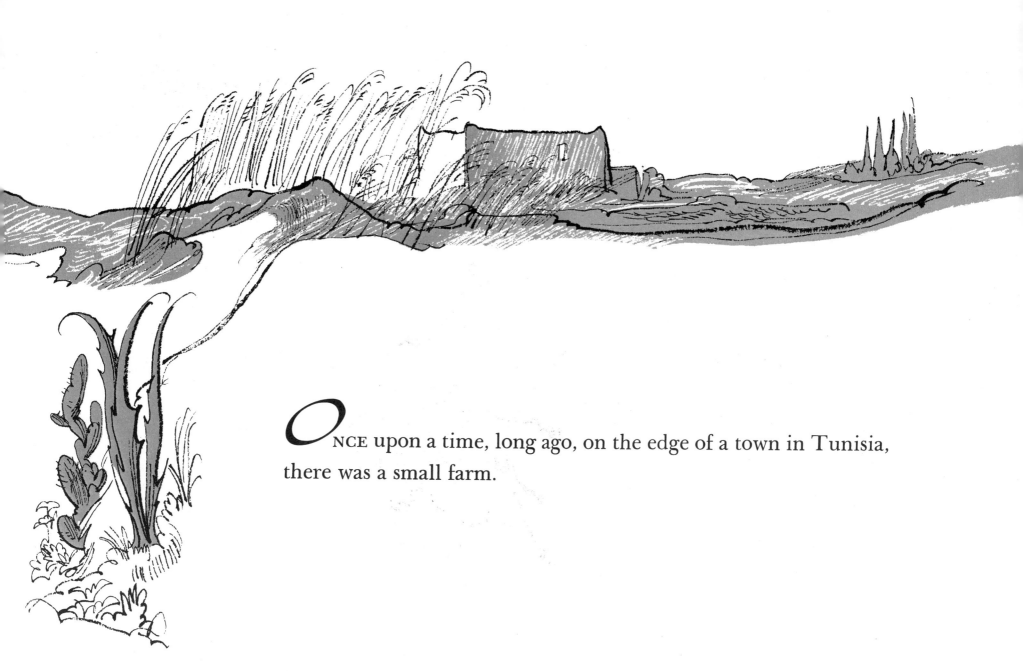

Once upon a time, long ago, on the edge of a town in Tunisia, there was a small farm.

The jackal and his friend, the hedgehog, lived on this small farm. Every morning they went out together to cultivate their wheat field.

They dug out all of the thorn bushes,

and carried away all of the stones scattered in the field.

Together they pulled up all of the weeds,
and planted the wheat.

When the wheat was ripe, it was time to harvest.

The hedgehog said, "We will have to divide the harvest, friend Jackal. I'll let you choose between what is in the ground and what is not."

The jackal, who was not very shrewd, answered, "I'll take what is in the ground."

So the jackal was left with nothing but the roots,

while the hedgehog trundled off
with the ripe wheat stalks.

The jackal was most unhappy and drank cup after cup of mint tea, in the town cafe, to console himself.

"I must never make the same mistake again," he muttered.

17

Soon it was time to plant the onions. The jackal and the hedgehog walked out to the field.

Together they carefully prepared the rows for planting.

The green stalks of the onions grew larger and taller each day.

Then the great heat came.

The stalks turned dry and yellow.

The hedgehog said to the jackal, "It's time to divide our harvest. Again I will let you choose first."

25

"This time," said the jackal, "I won't let you fool me. I'll take what is above the ground!"

So the jackal eagerly cut the stalks for himself,

while the hedgehog carried off the rest.

The jackal, seeing that he had been fooled again, walked angrily away from the farm with his tail between his legs.

31

And that is why to this day the jackal
will not speak to the hedgehog.